[redacted]

STAR WARS®

EPISODE III

REVENGE OF THE SITH

VOLUME THREE

ADAPTED FROM THE STORY
AND SCREENPLAY BY
GEORGE LUCAS

SCRIPT
MILES LANE

ART
DOUGLAS WHEATLEY

COLORS
CHRIS CHUCKRY

LETTERING
MICHAEL DAVID THOMAS

COVER ART
DAVE DORMAN

Anakin Skywalker is plagued by nightmares in which his wife Padmé dies during childbirth. Compounding his stress is Chancellor Palpatine's appointment of him as his personal representative to the Jedi Council. The Council reluctantly accepts Anakin, but in turn asks him to report on the actions of Palpatine, whom the Jedi no longer trust.

Padmé also questions the Chancellor's actions and joins Senators Bail Organa and Mon Mothma in planning an opposition to Palpatine. Later, Padmé tries to discuss the subject with Anakin, but he is too obsessed with preventing her death to pay attention. Palpatine fuels his obsession further, telling him of a Sith Lord who discovered how to prevent those he cared about from dying.

Obi-Wan Kenobi confronts Separatist leader General Grievous on Utapau, and kills him. Anakin had wanted to join Obi-Wan in the attack, but he was ordered to remain on Coruscant to report on Palpatine's reaction to Grievous's death. Palpatine does make a startling revelation to Anakin . . .

[redacted]

DARK HORSE COMICS

Spotlight

VISIT US AT
www.abdopublishing.com

Reinforced library bound edition published in 2010 by Spotlight, a division of the ABDO Group, 8000 West 78th Street, Edina, Minnesota 55439. Spotlight produces high-quality reinforced library bound editions for schools and libraries. Published by agreement with Dark Horse Comics, Inc., and Lucasfilm Ltd.

Library of Congress Cataloging-in-Publication Data

Lane, Miles.
  Star wars, episode III, revenge of the Sith / based on the story and screenplay by George Lucas ; Miles Lane, adaptation ; Doug Wheatley, art ; Chris Chuckry, colors ; Michael David Thomas, letters. -- Reinforced library bound ed.
    v. <1-4> cm.
  "Dark Horse."
  ISBN 978-1-59961-617-9 (volume 1) -- ISBN 978-1-59961-618-6 (volume 2) -- ISBN 978-1-59961-619-3 (volume 3) -- ISBN 978-1-59961-620-9 (volume 4)
  I. Lucas, George, 1944- II. Wheatley, Doug. III. Chuckry, Chris. IV. Thomas, Michael David. V. Dark Horse Comics. VI. Star Wars, episode III, revenge of the Sith (Motion picture) VII. Title. VIII. Title: Star wars, episode three, revenge of the Sith. IX. Title: Star wars, episode 3, revenge of the Sith. X. Title: Revenge of the Sith.
  PZ7.7.L36Std 2009
  741.5'973--dc22

                    2009002014

All Spotlight books have reinforced library bindings and
are manufactured in the United States of America.

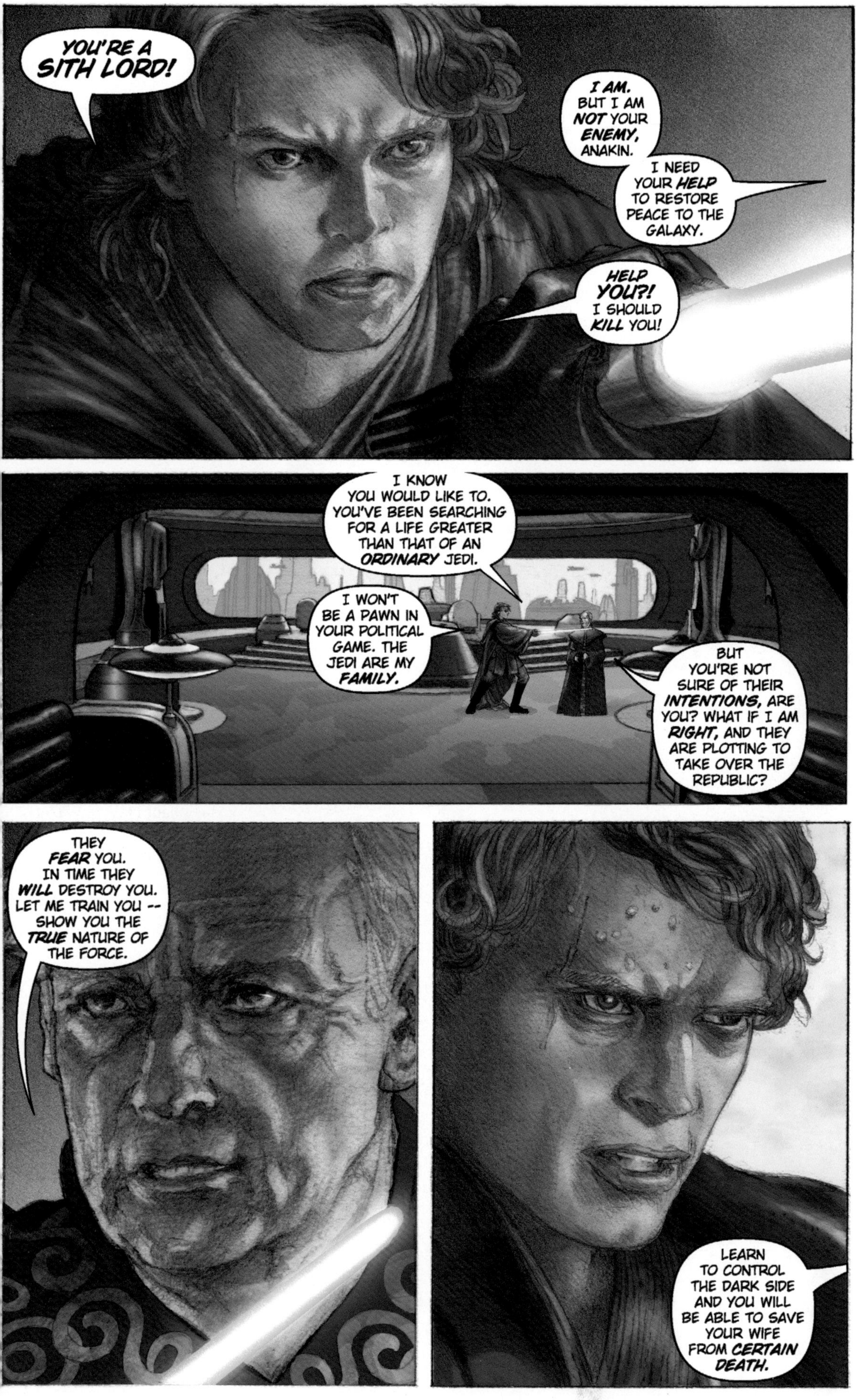
YOU'RE A SITH LORD!
I AM. BUT I AM NOT YOUR ENEMY, ANAKIN.
I NEED YOUR HELP TO RESTORE PEACE TO THE GALAXY.
HELP YOU?! I SHOULD KILL YOU!
I KNOW YOU WOULD LIKE TO. YOU'VE BEEN SEARCHING FOR A LIFE GREATER THAN THAT OF AN ORDINARY JEDI.
I WON'T BE A PAWN IN YOUR POLITICAL GAME. THE JEDI ARE MY FAMILY.
BUT YOU'RE NOT SURE OF THEIR INTENTIONS, ARE YOU? WHAT IF I AM RIGHT, AND THEY ARE PLOTTING TO TAKE OVER THE REPUBLIC?
THEY FEAR YOU. IN TIME THEY WILL DESTROY YOU. LET ME TRAIN YOU -- SHOW YOU THE TRUE NATURE OF THE FORCE.
LEARN TO CONTROL THE DARK SIDE AND YOU WILL BE ABLE TO SAVE YOUR WIFE FROM CERTAIN DEATH.

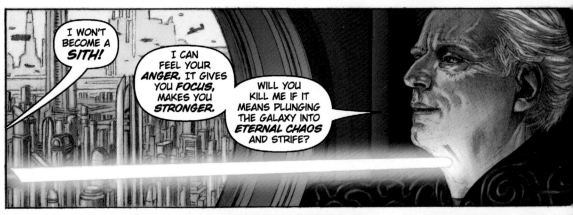

I WON'T BECOME A *SITH!*

I CAN FEEL YOUR *ANGER.* IT GIVES YOU *FOCUS,* MAKES YOU *STRONGER.*

WILL YOU KILL ME IF IT MEANS PLUNGING THE GALAXY INTO *ETERNAL CHAOS* AND STRIFE?

I AM GOING TO TURN YOU OVER TO THE JEDI COUNCIL ... I WILL DISCOVER THE *TRUTH* OF ALL THIS.

YOU HAVE *GREAT WISDOM,* ANAKIN. I WANT YOU TO MEDITATE ON MY PROPOSAL TO KNOW THE POWER OF THE DARK SIDE.

THE POWER TO *SAVE PADMÉ.*

UTAPAU.

SEND A MESSAGE TO CORUSCANT. GENERAL GRIEVOUS IS *DEAD.*

YES, SIR!

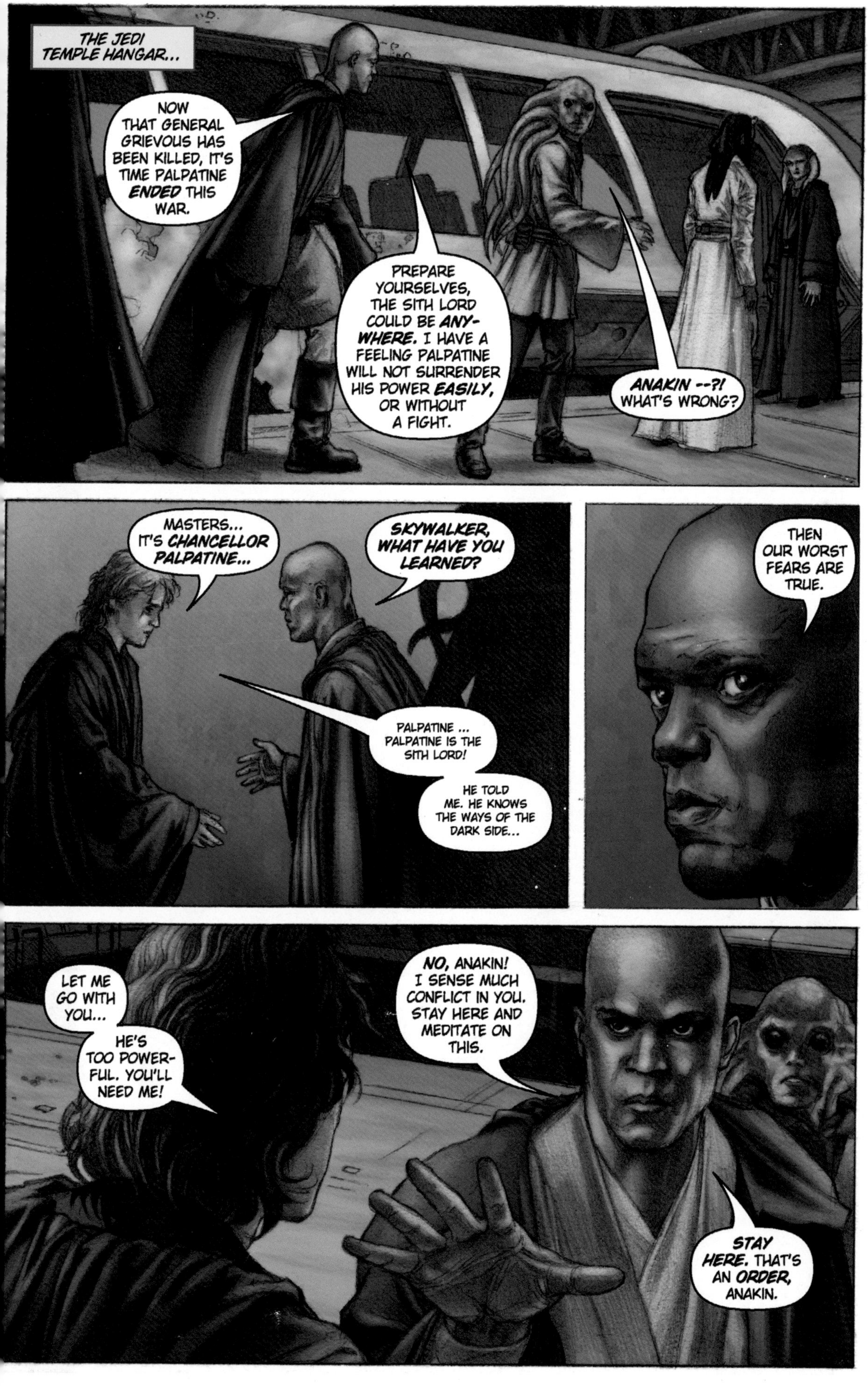
THE JEDI TEMPLE HANGAR...
NOW THAT GENERAL GRIEVOUS HAS BEEN KILLED, IT'S TIME PALPATINE ENDED THIS WAR.
PREPARE YOURSELVES, THE SITH LORD COULD BE ANY-WHERE. I HAVE A FEELING PALPATINE WILL NOT SURRENDER HIS POWER EASILY, OR WITHOUT A FIGHT.
ANAKIN --?! WHAT'S WRONG?
MASTERS... IT'S CHANCELLOR PALPATINE...
SKYWALKER, WHAT HAVE YOU LEARNED?
PALPATINE ... PALPATINE IS THE SITH LORD!
HE TOLD ME. HE KNOWS THE WAYS OF THE DARK SIDE...
THEN OUR WORST FEARS ARE TRUE.
LET ME GO WITH YOU...
HE'S TOO POWER-FUL. YOU'LL NEED ME!
NO, ANAKIN! I SENSE MUCH CONFLICT IN YOU. STAY HERE AND MEDITATE ON THIS.
STAY HERE. THAT'S AN ORDER, ANAKIN.

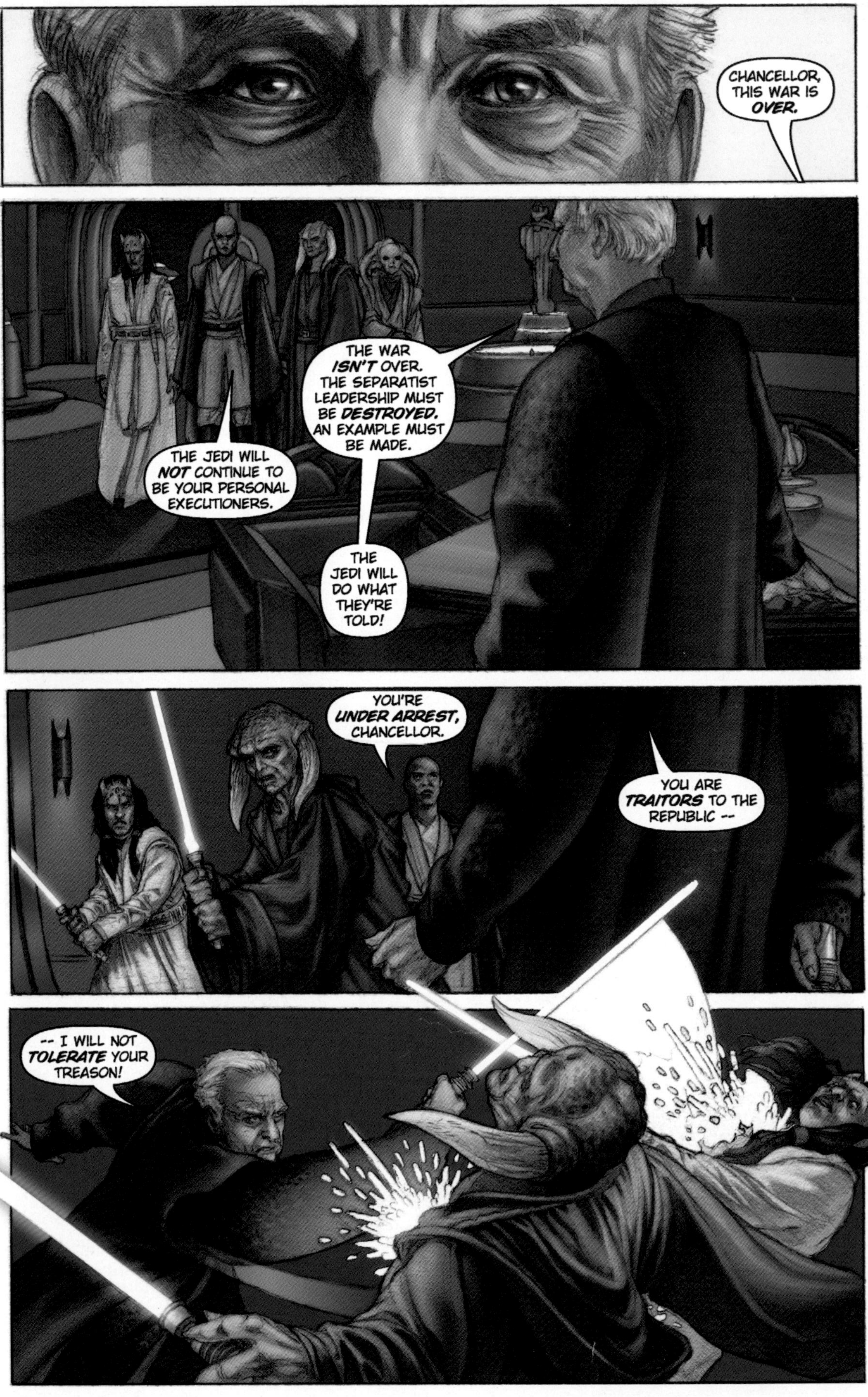
CHANCELLOR, THIS WAR IS OVER.
THE JEDI WILL NOT CONTINUE TO BE YOUR PERSONAL EXECUTIONERS.
THE WAR ISN'T OVER. THE SEPARATIST LEADERSHIP MUST BE DESTROYED. AN EXAMPLE MUST BE MADE.
THE JEDI WILL DO WHAT THEY'RE TOLD!
YOU'RE UNDER ARREST, CHANCELLOR.
YOU ARE TRAITORS TO THE REPUBLIC --
-- I WILL NOT TOLERATE YOUR TREASON!

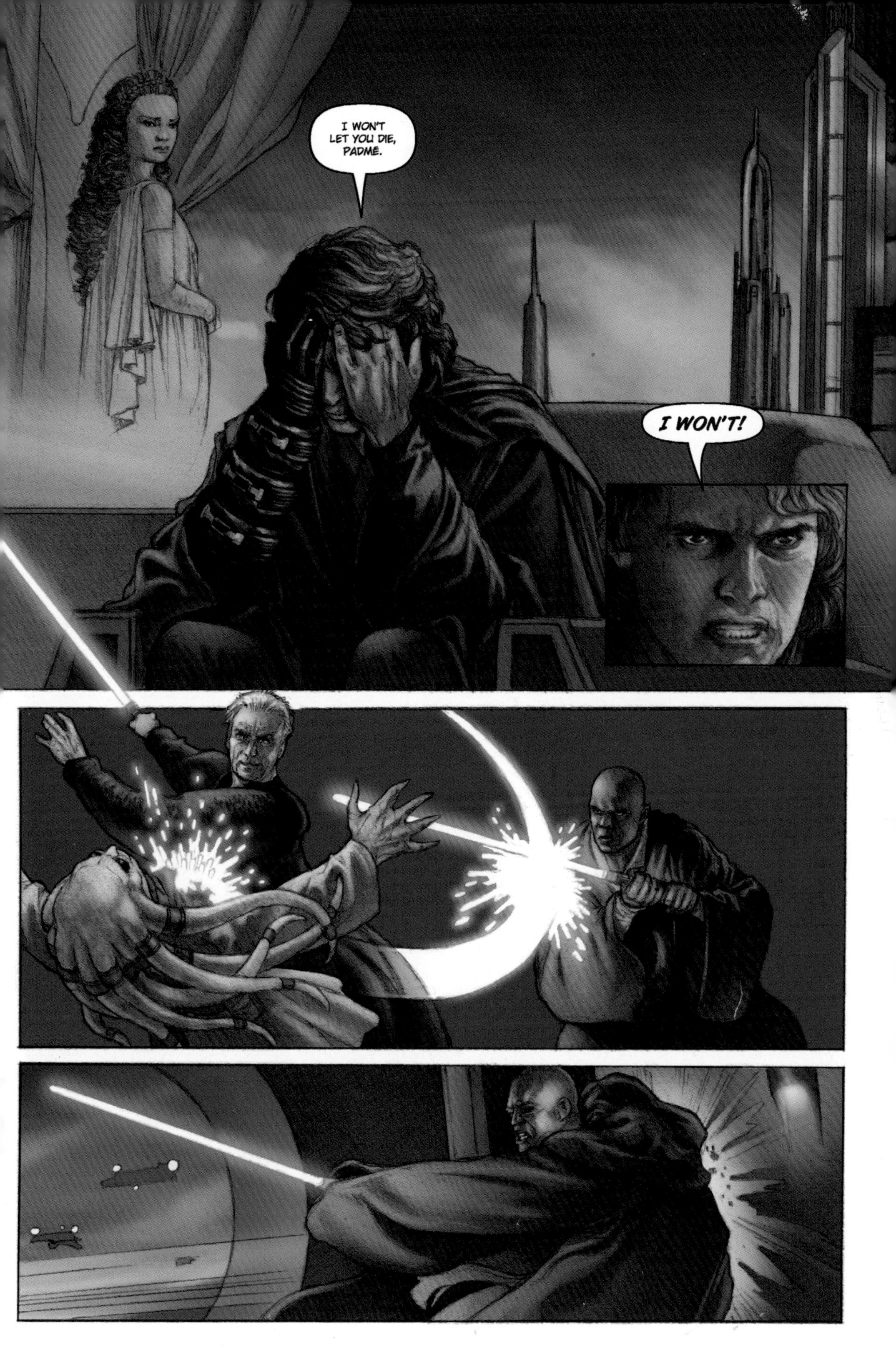
I WON'T LET YOU DIE, PADMÉ.
I WON'T!

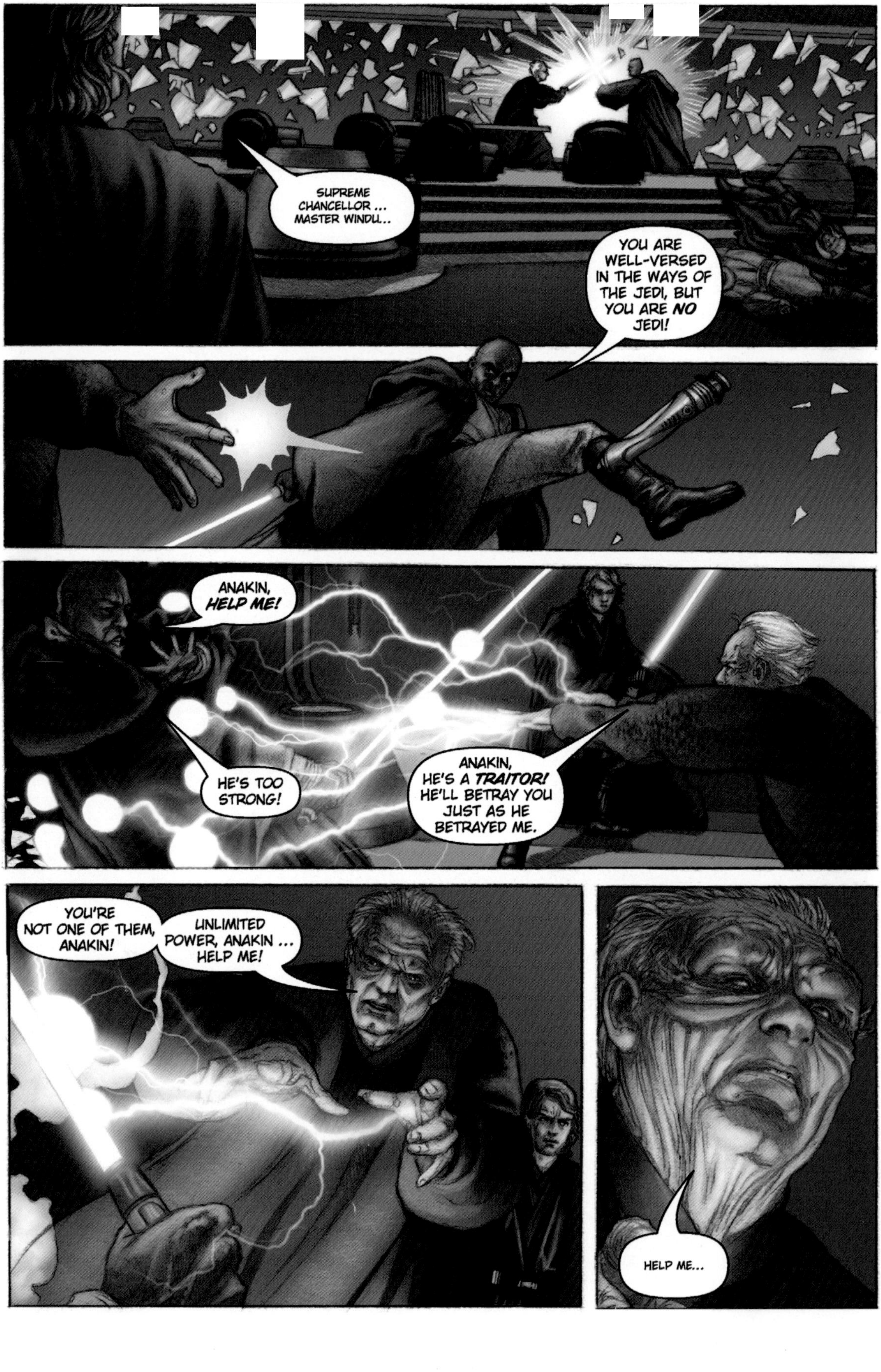
SUPREME CHANCELLOR ... MASTER WINDU...
YOU ARE WELL-VERSED IN THE WAYS OF THE JEDI, BUT YOU ARE *NO* JEDI!
ANAKIN, *HELP ME!*
HE'S TOO STRONG!
ANAKIN, HE'S A *TRAITOR!* HE'LL BETRAY YOU JUST AS HE BETRAYED ME.
YOU'RE NOT ONE OF THEM, ANAKIN!
UNLIMITED POWER, ANAKIN ... HELP ME!
HELP ME...

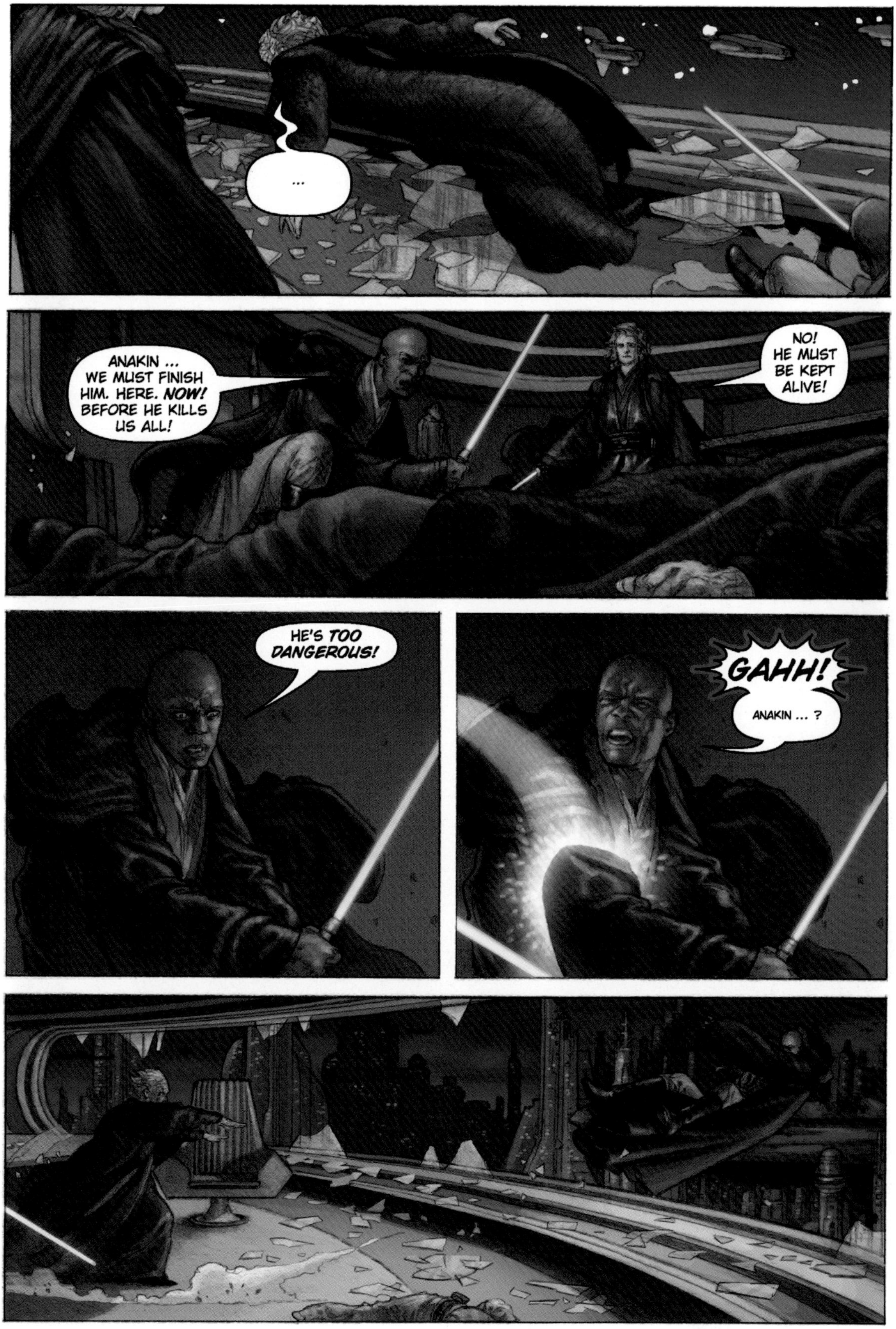
...
ANAKIN ... WE MUST FINISH HIM. HERE. NOW! BEFORE HE KILLS US ALL!
NO! HE MUST BE KEPT ALIVE!
HE'S TOO DANGEROUS!
GAHH!
ANAKIN ... ?

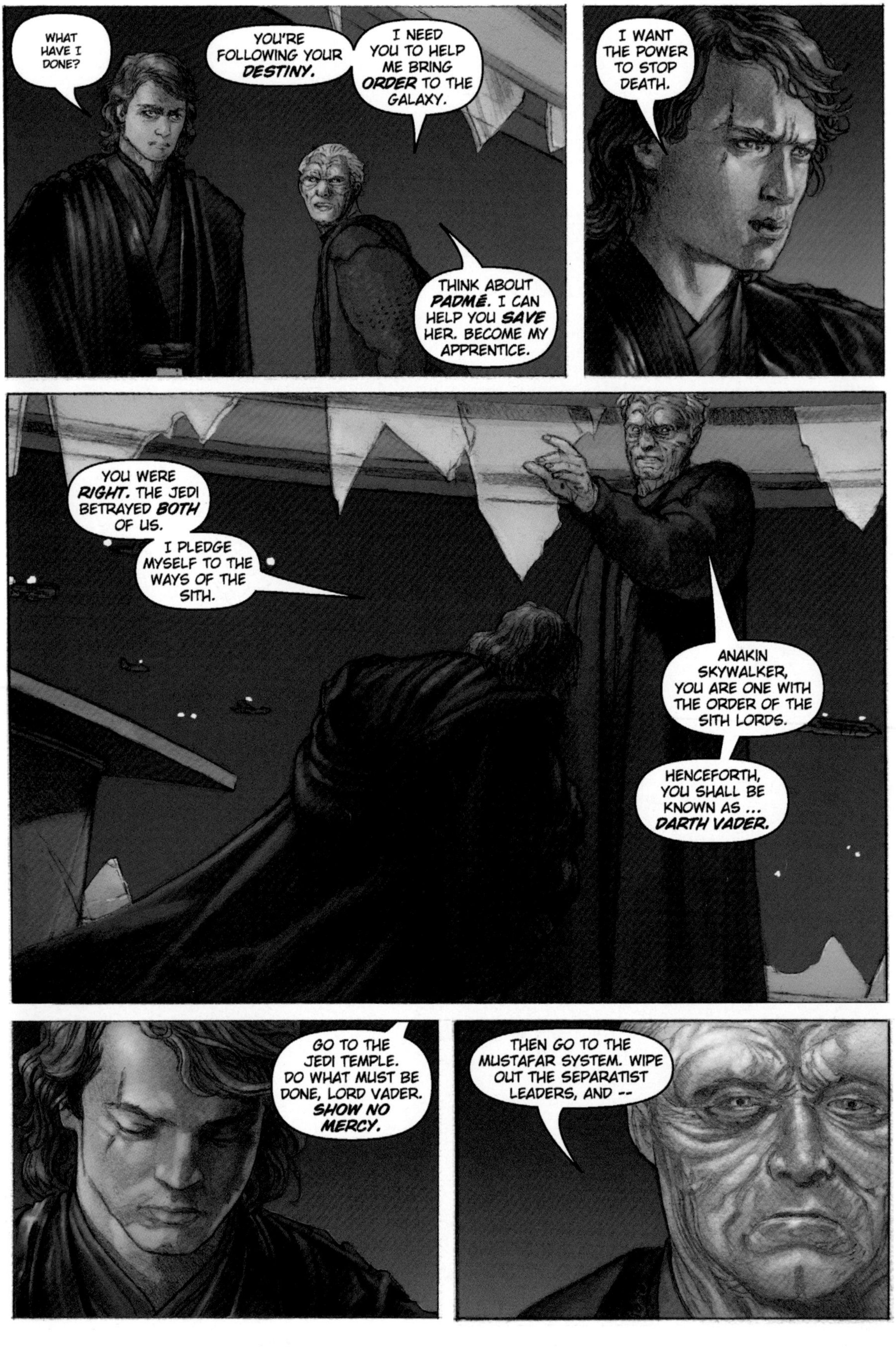
WHAT HAVE I DONE?
YOU'RE FOLLOWING YOUR **DESTINY.**
I NEED YOU TO HELP ME BRING **ORDER** TO THE GALAXY.
THINK ABOUT **PADMÉ.** I CAN HELP YOU **SAVE** HER. BECOME MY APPRENTICE.
I WANT THE POWER TO STOP DEATH.
YOU WERE **RIGHT.** THE JEDI BETRAYED **BOTH** OF US.
I PLEDGE MYSELF TO THE WAYS OF THE SITH.
ANAKIN SKYWALKER, YOU ARE ONE WITH THE ORDER OF THE SITH LORDS.
HENCEFORTH, YOU SHALL BE KNOWN AS ... **DARTH VADER.**
GO TO THE JEDI TEMPLE. DO WHAT MUST BE DONE, LORD VADER. **SHOW NO MERCY.**
THEN GO TO THE MUSTAFAR SYSTEM. WIPE OUT THE SEPARATIST LEADERS, AND --

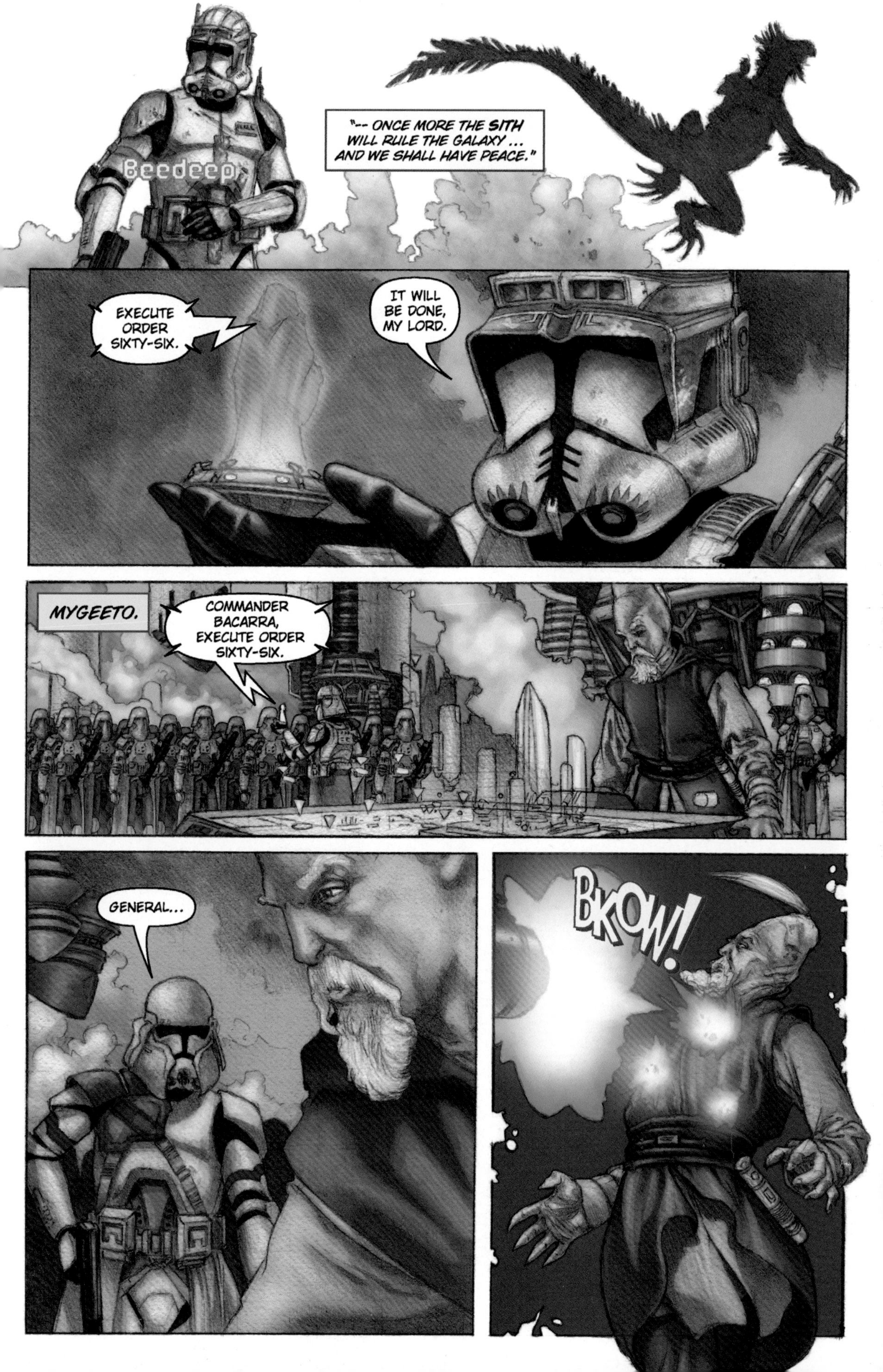
Beedeep
"-- ONCE MORE THE SITH WILL RULE THE GALAXY ... AND WE SHALL HAVE PEACE."
EXECUTE ORDER SIXTY-SIX.
IT WILL BE DONE, MY LORD.
MYGEETO.
COMMANDER BACARRA, EXECUTE ORDER SIXTY-SIX.
GENERAL...
BKOW!

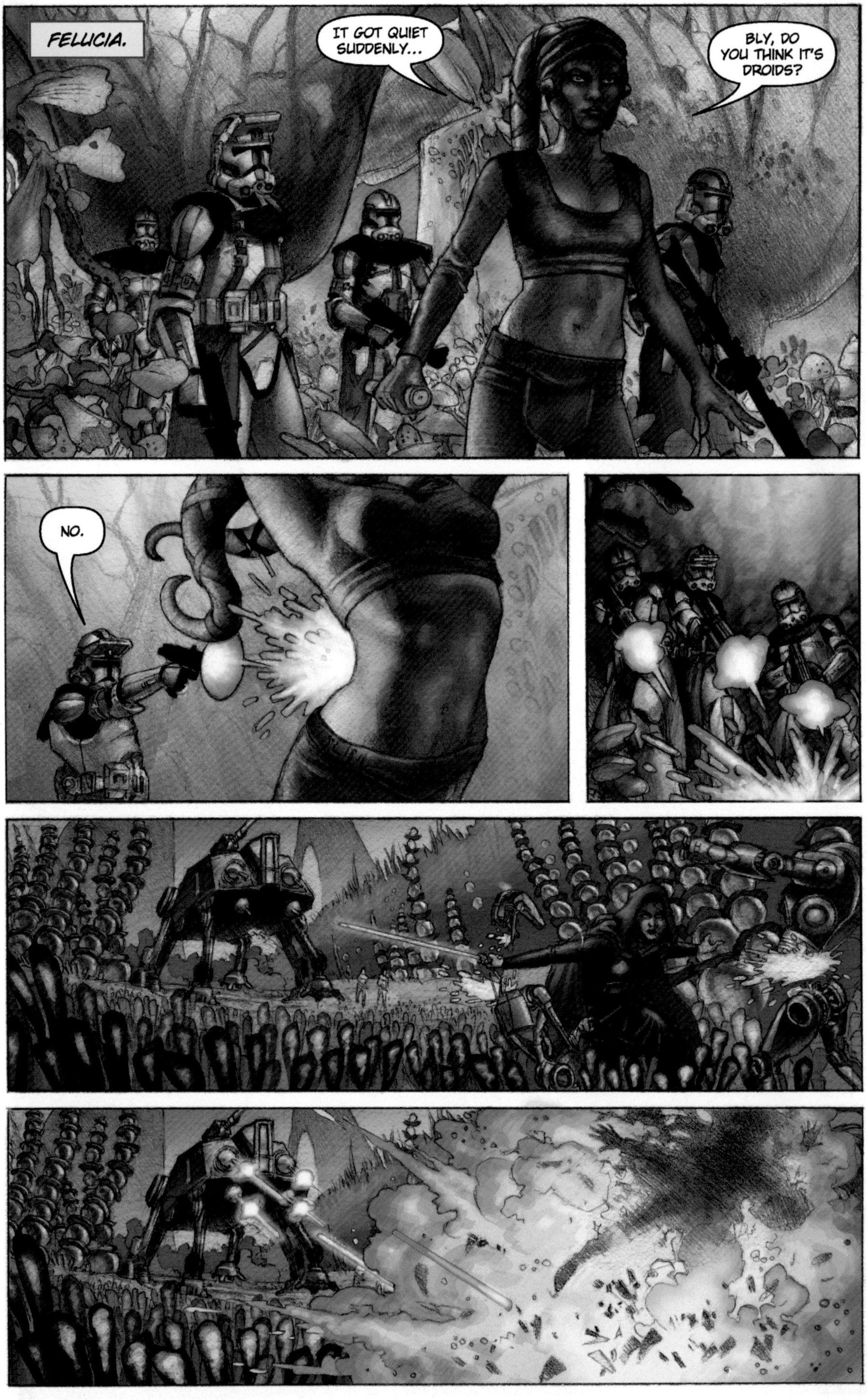
FELUCIA.
IT GOT QUIET SUDDENLY...
BLY, DO YOU THINK IT'S DROIDS?
NO.

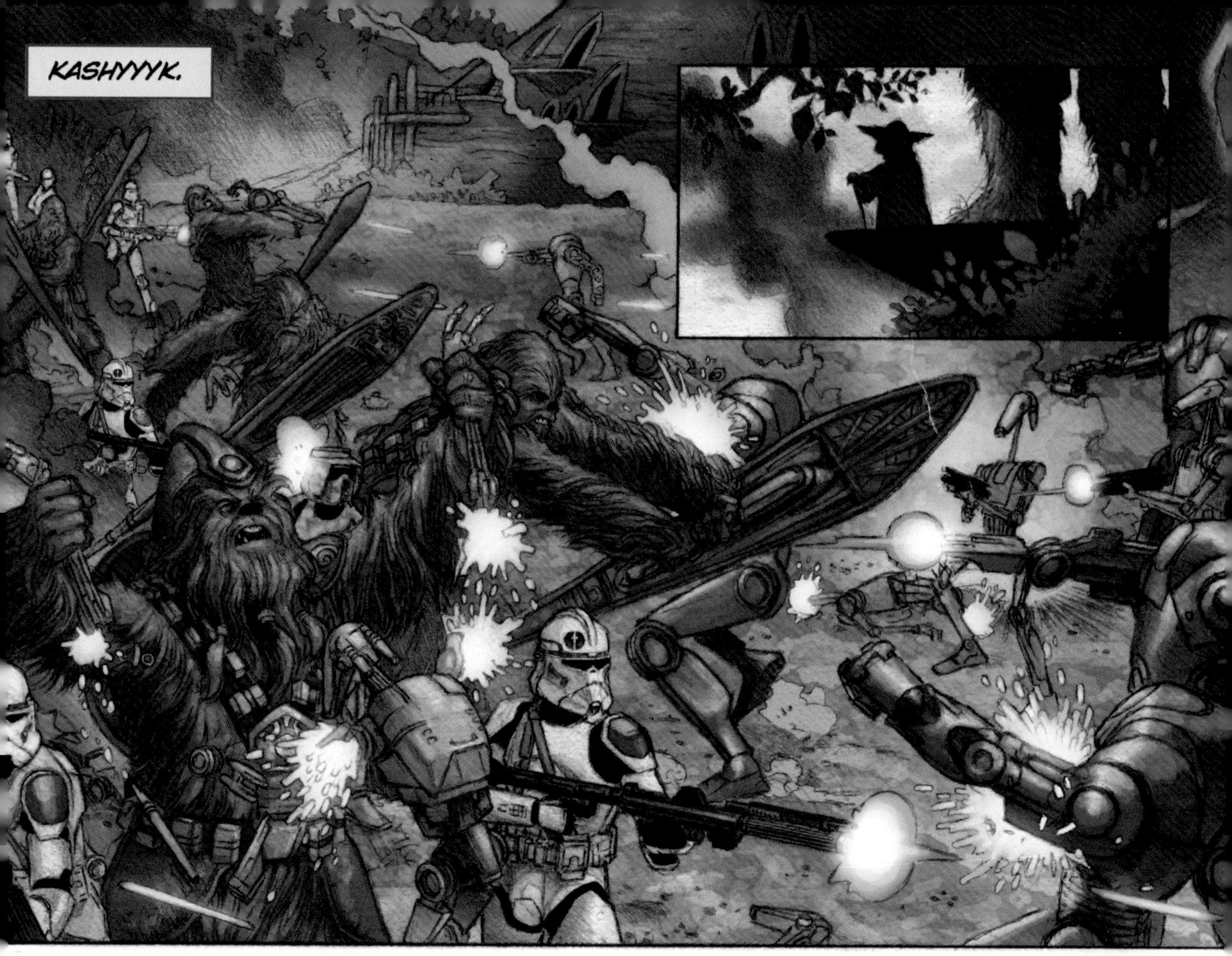
KASHYYYK.

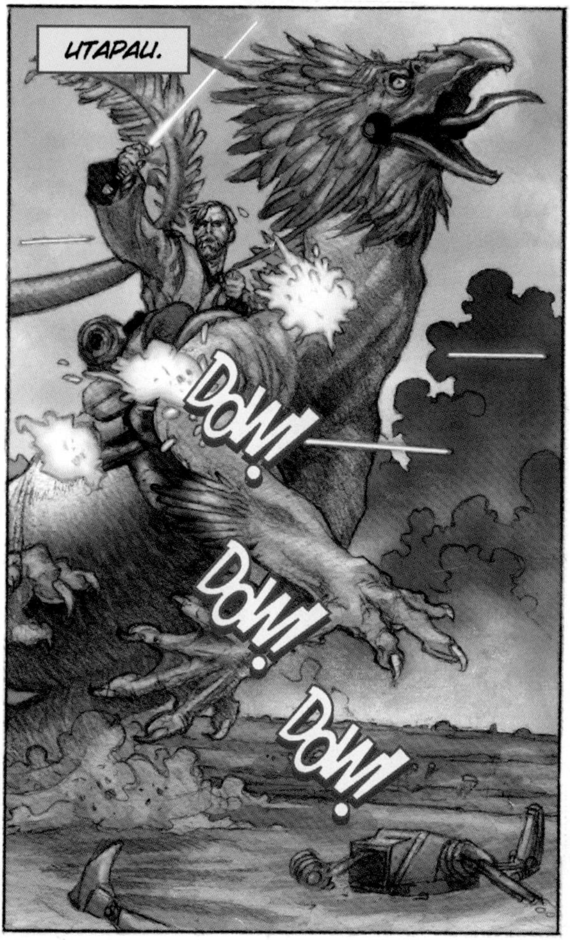
UTAPAU.
DOW!
DOW!
DOW!

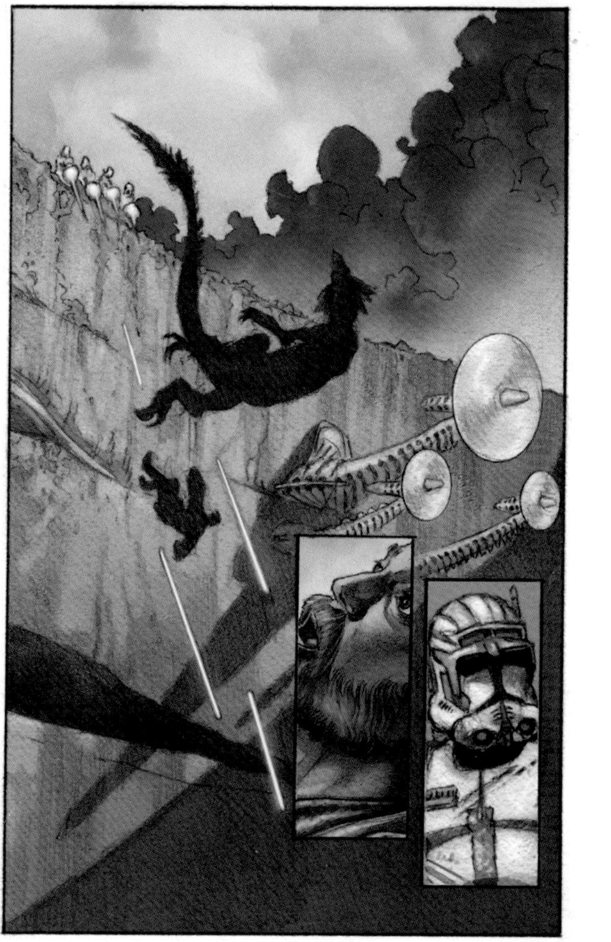

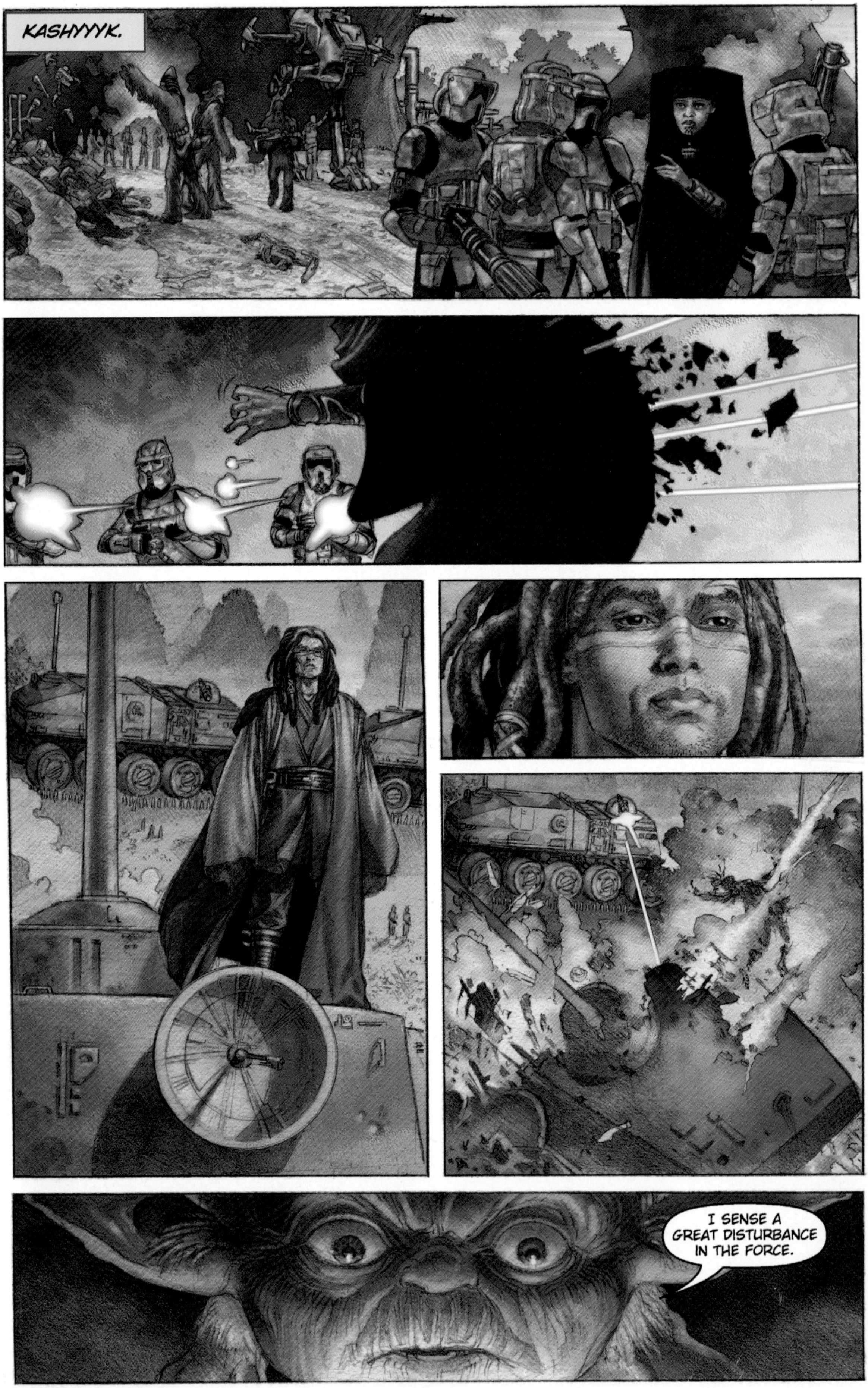
KASHYYYK.
I SENSE A GREAT DISTURBANCE IN THE FORCE.

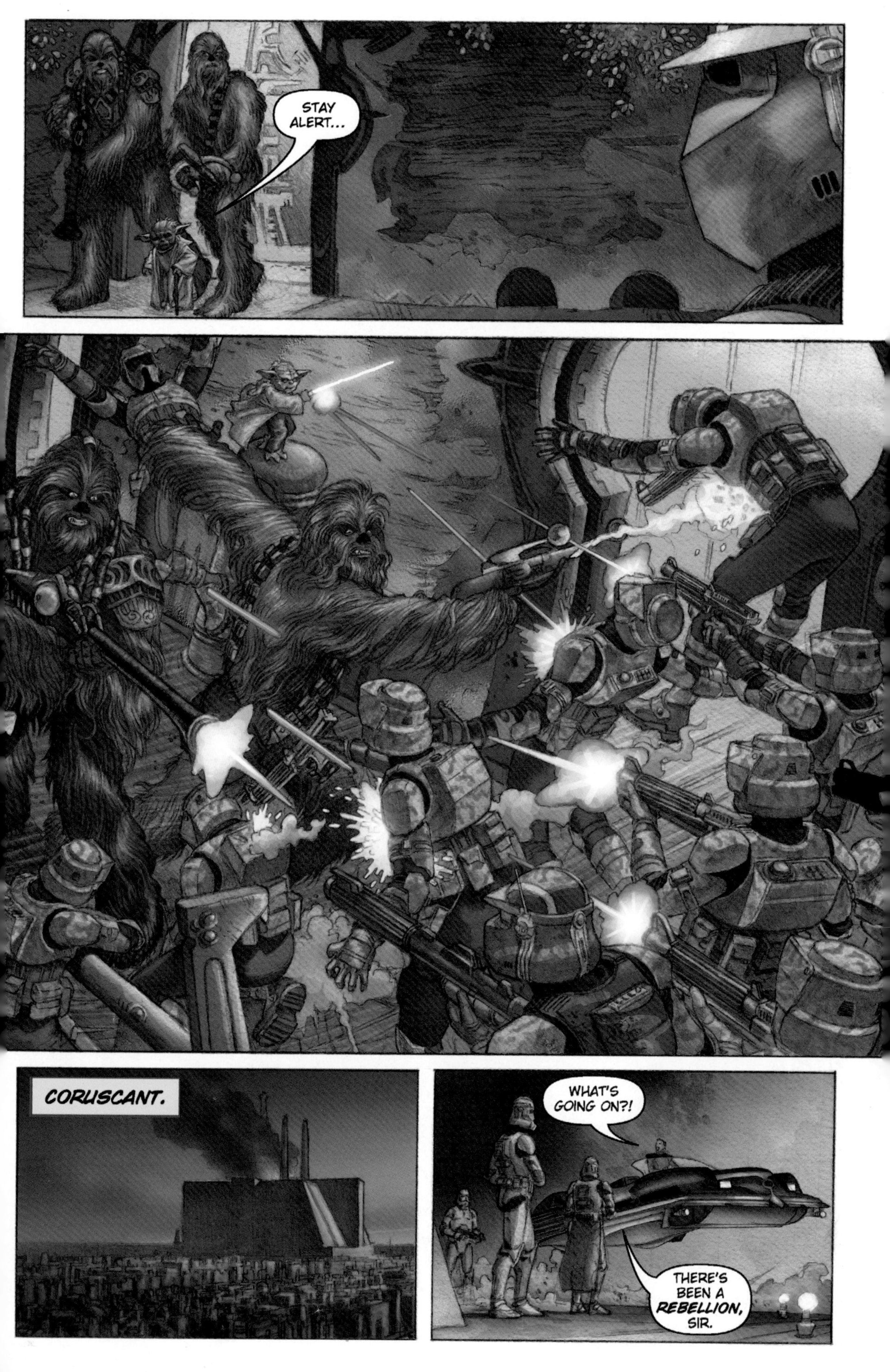
STAY ALERT...
CORUSCANT.
WHAT'S GOING ON?!
THERE'S BEEN A *REBELLION,* SIR.

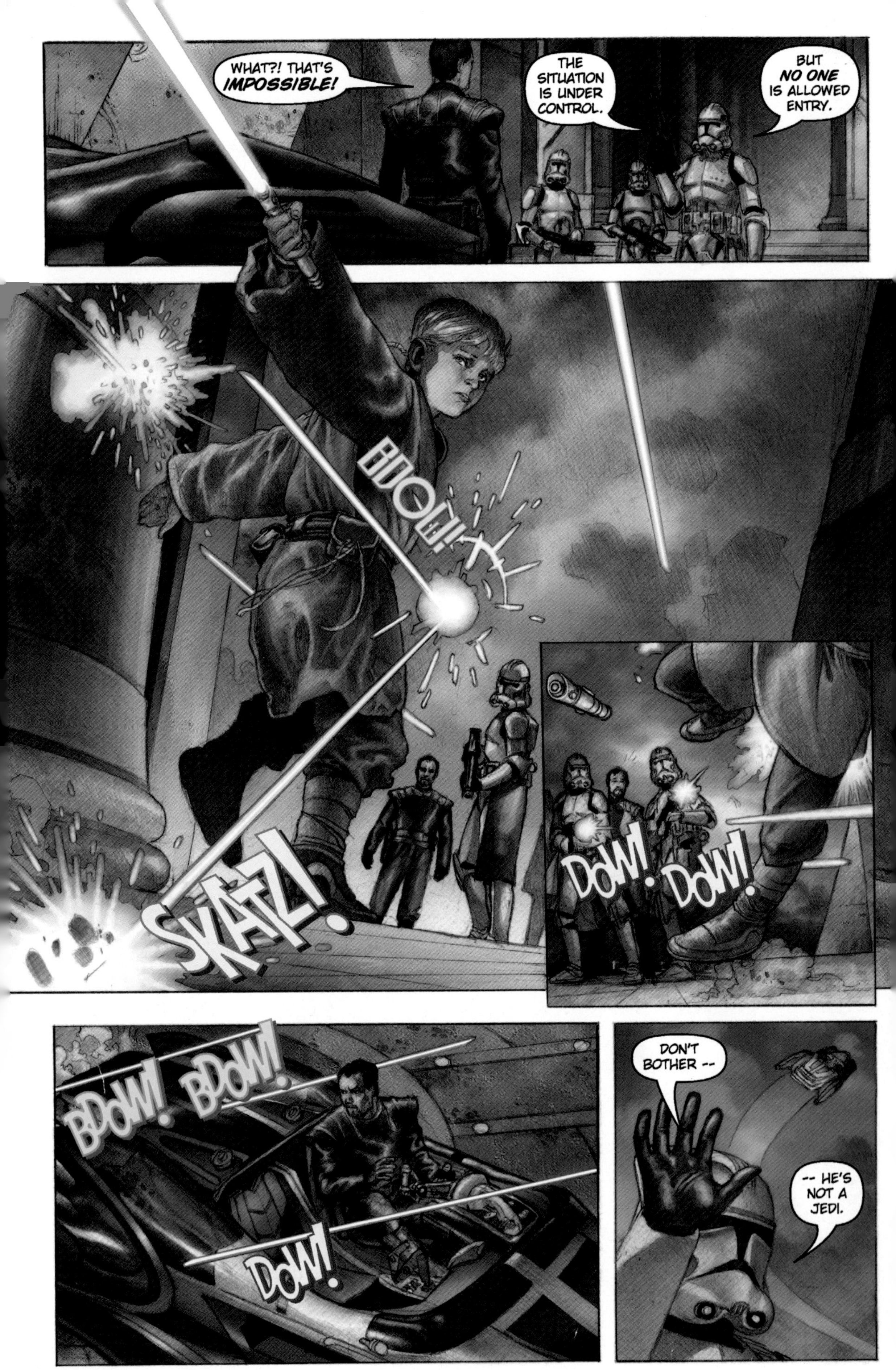
WHAT?! THAT'S IMPOSSIBLE!
THE SITUATION IS UNDER CONTROL.
BUT NO ONE IS ALLOWED ENTRY.
BDOOM!
SKATZ!
DOW! DOW!
BDOW! BDOW!
DOW!
DON'T BOTHER --
-- HE'S NOT A JEDI.

MY LADY, THERE'S A *JEDI FIGHTER* DOCKING ON THE VERANDA.

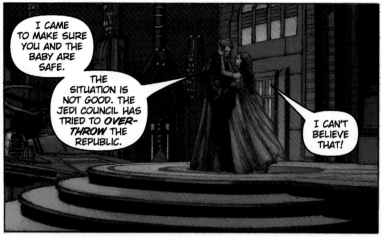

I CAME TO MAKE SURE YOU AND THE BABY ARE SAFE.

THE SITUATION IS NOT GOOD. THE JEDI COUNCIL HAS TRIED TO *OVER-THROW* THE REPUBLIC.

I CAN'T BELIEVE THAT!

I SAW MASTER WINDU ATTEMPT TO ASSASSINATE THE CHANCELLOR MYSELF.

W-WHAT ARE YOU GOING TO DO?

I WILL *NOT* BETRAY THE REPUBLIC. MY LOYALTIES LIE WITH THE CHANCELLOR AND THE SENATE ... AND WITH *YOU.*

WHAT ABOUT OBI-WAN?

I DON'T KNOW ... MANY OF THE JEDI HAVE BEEN KILLED.

HOW COULD THIS HAVE HAPPENED?

THE REPUBLIC IS UNSTABLE, PADME. THE JEDI AREN'T THE ONLY ONES TRYING TO TAKE ADVANTAGE OF THE SITUATION.

THERE ARE ALSO TRAITORS IN THE *SENATE.*

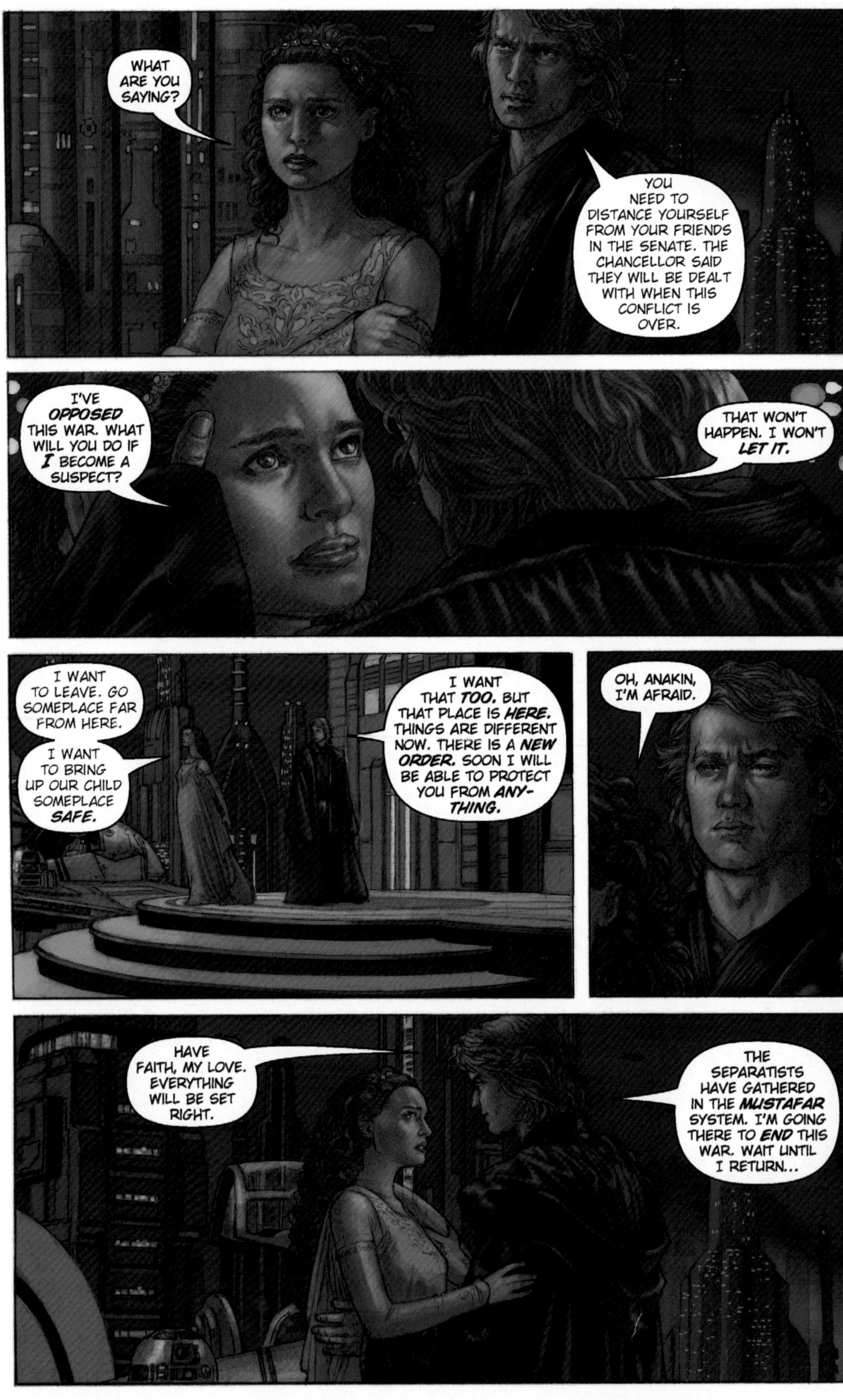

WHAT ARE YOU SAYING?
YOU NEED TO DISTANCE YOURSELF FROM YOUR FRIENDS IN THE SENATE. THE CHANCELLOR SAID THEY WILL BE DEALT WITH WHEN THIS CONFLICT IS OVER.
I'VE ***OPPOSED*** THIS WAR. WHAT WILL YOU DO IF ***I*** BECOME A SUSPECT?
THAT WON'T HAPPEN. I WON'T ***LET IT.***
I WANT TO LEAVE. GO SOMEPLACE FAR FROM HERE.
I WANT TO BRING UP OUR CHILD SOMEPLACE ***SAFE.***
I WANT THAT ***TOO.*** BUT THAT PLACE IS ***HERE.*** THINGS ARE DIFFERENT NOW. THERE IS A ***NEW ORDER.*** SOON I WILL BE ABLE TO PROTECT YOU FROM ***ANY-THING.***
OH, ANAKIN, I'M AFRAID.
HAVE FAITH, MY LOVE. EVERYTHING WILL BE SET RIGHT.
THE SEPARATISTS HAVE GATHERED IN THE ***MUSTAFAR*** SYSTEM. I'M GOING THERE TO ***END*** THIS WAR. WAIT UNTIL I RETURN...

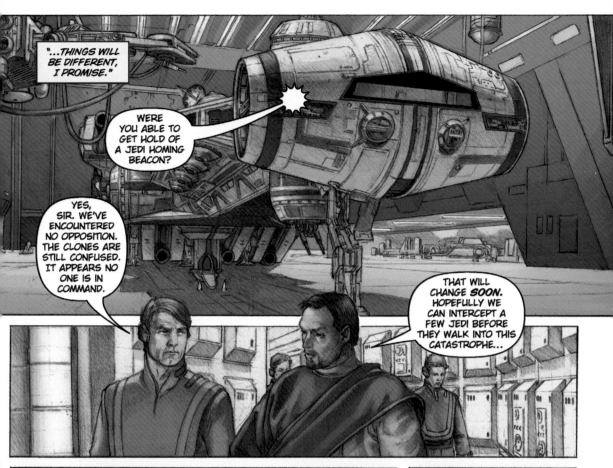

"...THINGS WILL BE DIFFERENT, I PROMISE."

WERE YOU ABLE TO GET HOLD OF A JEDI HOMING BEACON?

YES, SIR. WE'VE ENCOUNTERED NO OPPOSITION. THE CLONES ARE STILL CONFUSED. IT APPEARS NO ONE IS IN COMMAND.

THAT WILL CHANGE *SOON*. HOPEFULLY WE CAN INTERCEPT A FEW JEDI BEFORE THEY WALK INTO THIS CATASTROPHE...

CHEWBACCA AND TARFFUL, *GOOD FRIENDS* ARE. FOR YOUR HELP, MUCH GRATITUDE AND RESPECT, I HAVE.

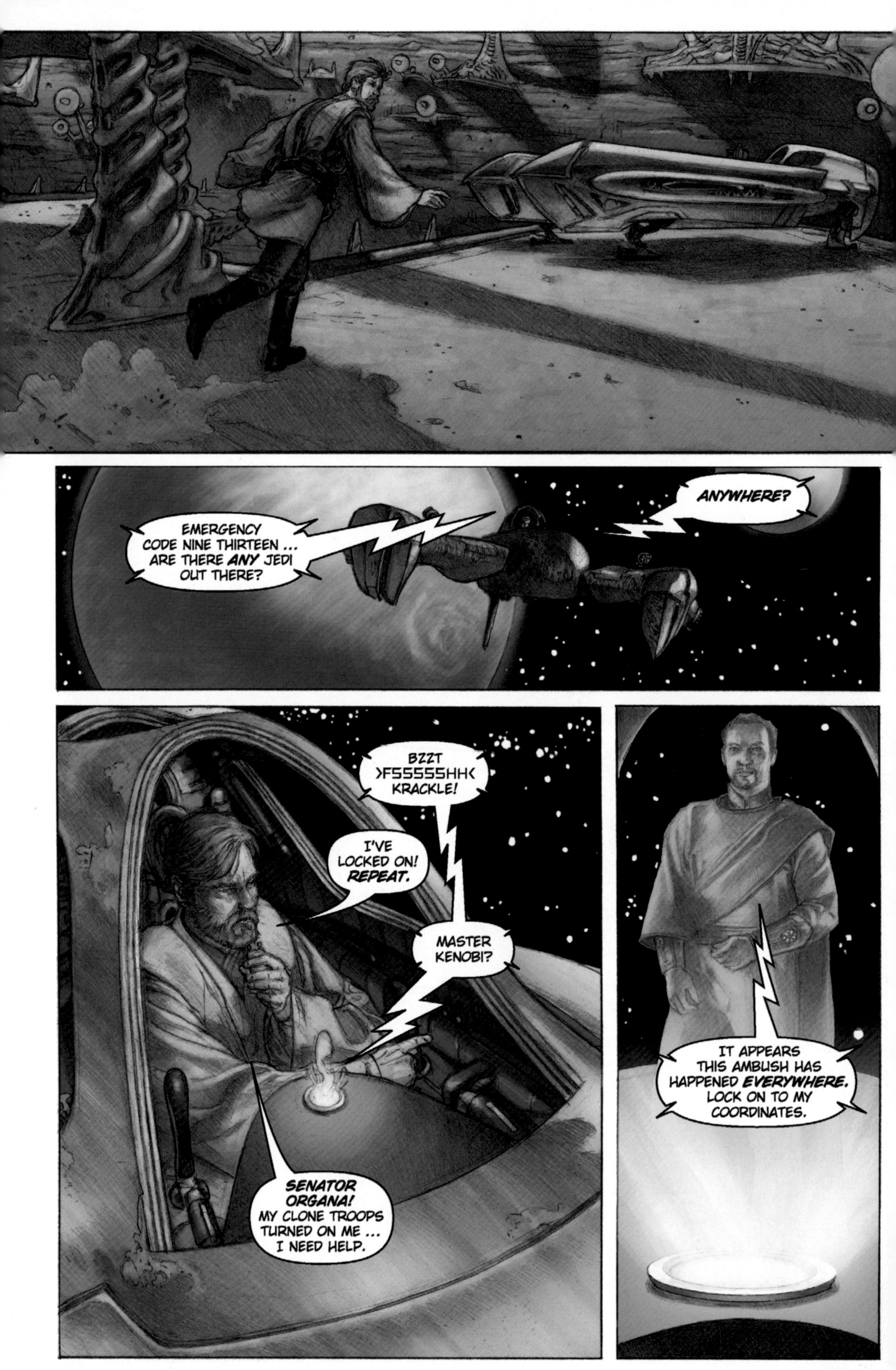
EMERGENCY CODE NINE THIRTEEN ... ARE THERE *ANY* JEDI OUT THERE?
ANYWHERE?
BZZT >FSSSSSHH< KRACKLE!
I'VE LOCKED ON! *REPEAT.*
MASTER KENOBI?
SENATOR ORGANA! MY CLONE TROOPS TURNED ON ME ... I NEED HELP.
IT APPEARS THIS AMBUSH HAS HAPPENED *EVERYWHERE.* LOCK ON TO MY COORDINATES.

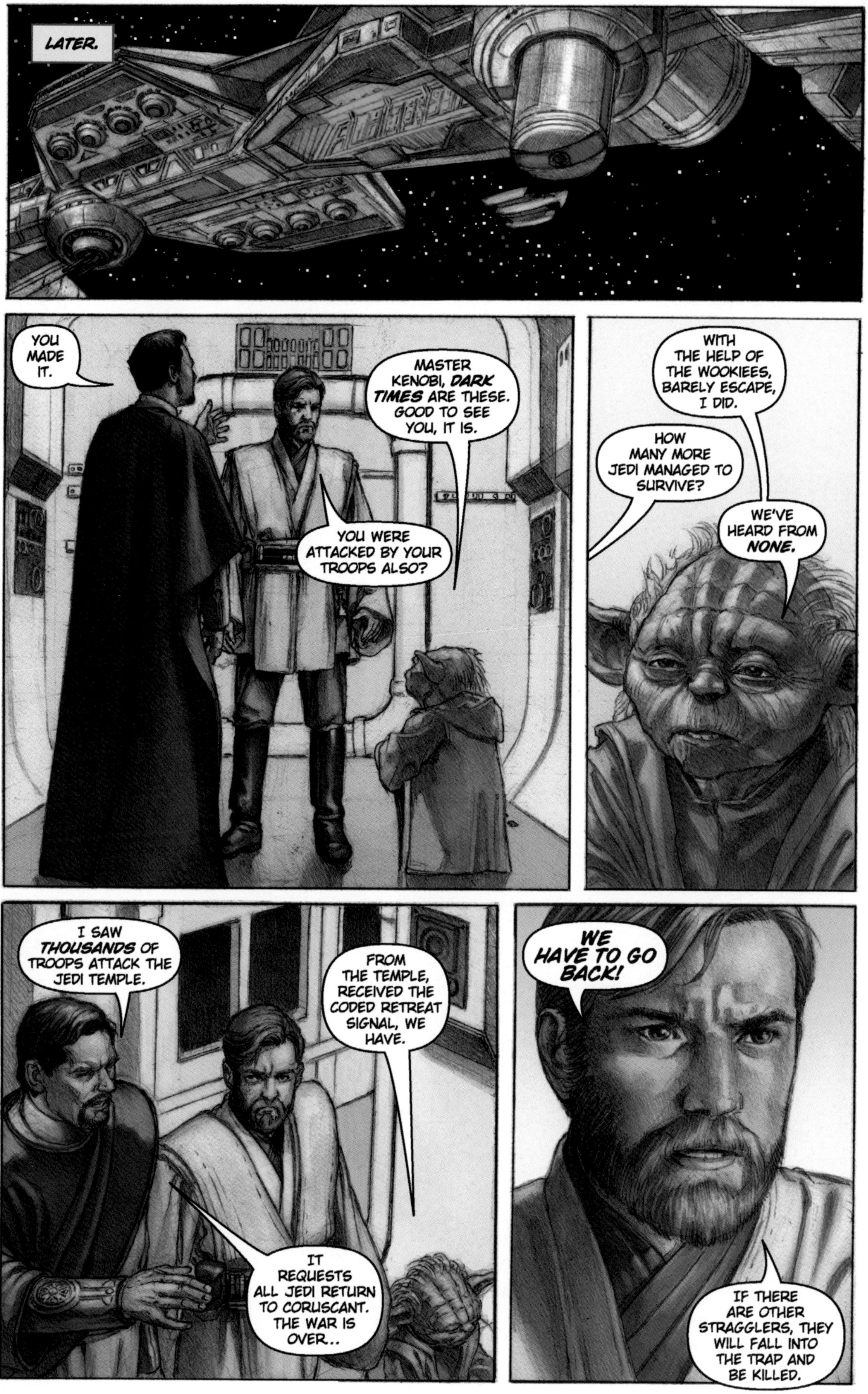
LATER.
YOU MADE IT.
MASTER KENOBI, DARK TIMES ARE THESE. GOOD TO SEE YOU, IT IS.
YOU WERE ATTACKED BY YOUR TROOPS ALSO?
WITH THE HELP OF THE WOOKIEES, BARELY ESCAPE, I DID.
HOW MANY MORE JEDI MANAGED TO SURVIVE?
WE'VE HEARD FROM NONE.
I SAW THOUSANDS OF TROOPS ATTACK THE JEDI TEMPLE.
FROM THE TEMPLE, RECEIVED THE CODED RETREAT SIGNAL, WE HAVE.
IT REQUESTS ALL JEDI RETURN TO CORUSCANT. THE WAR IS OVER..
WE HAVE TO GO BACK!
IF THERE ARE OTHER STRAGGLERS, THEY WILL FALL INTO THE TRAP AND BE KILLED.

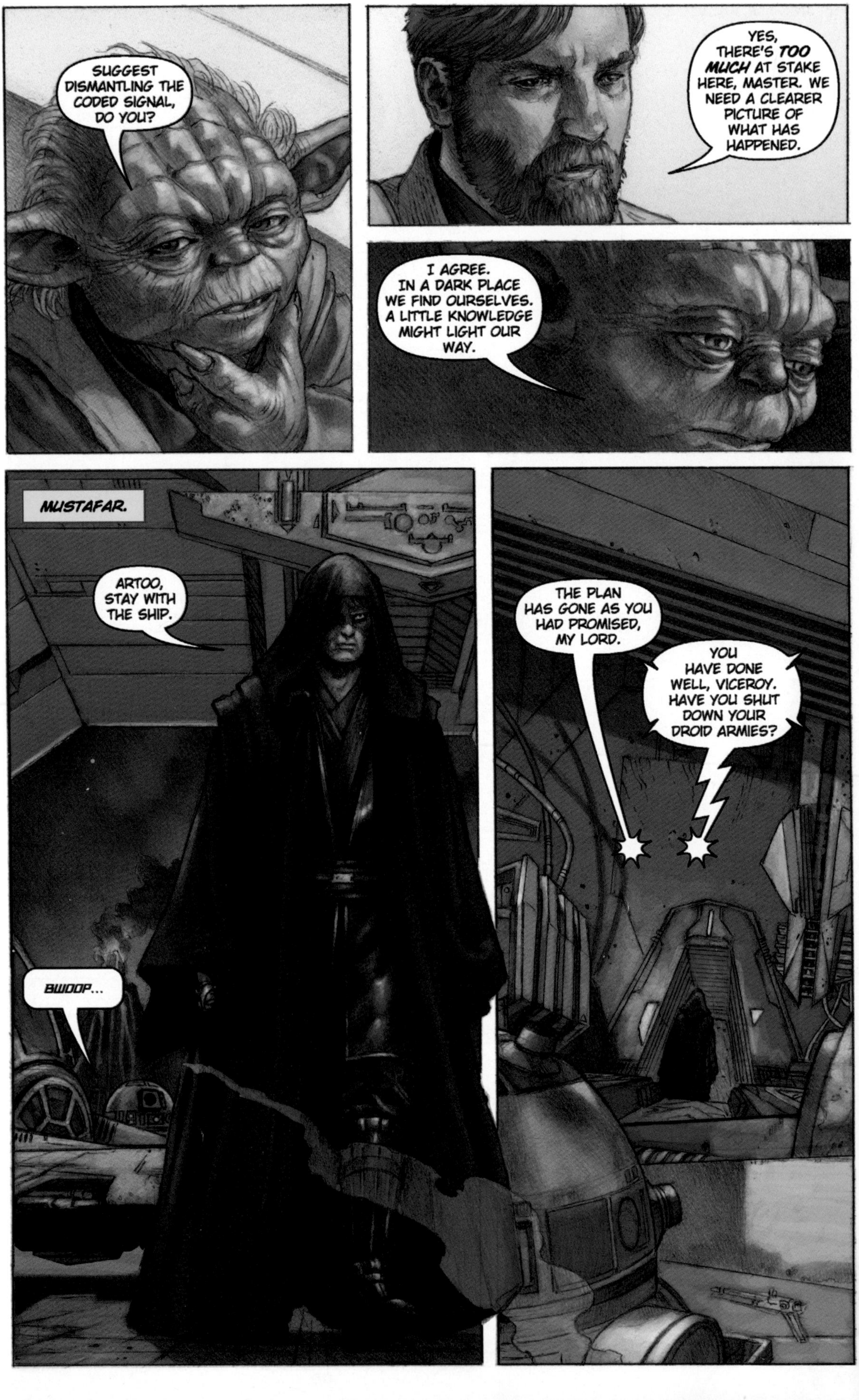
SUGGEST DISMANTLING THE CODED SIGNAL, DO YOU?
YES, THERE'S TOO MUCH AT STAKE HERE, MASTER. WE NEED A CLEARER PICTURE OF WHAT HAS HAPPENED.
I AGREE. IN A DARK PLACE WE FIND OURSELVES. A LITTLE KNOWLEDGE MIGHT LIGHT OUR WAY.
MUSTAFAR.
ARTOO, STAY WITH THE SHIP.
BWOOP...
THE PLAN HAS GONE AS YOU HAD PROMISED, MY LORD.
YOU HAVE DONE WELL, VICEROY. HAVE YOU SHUT DOWN YOUR DROID ARMIES?

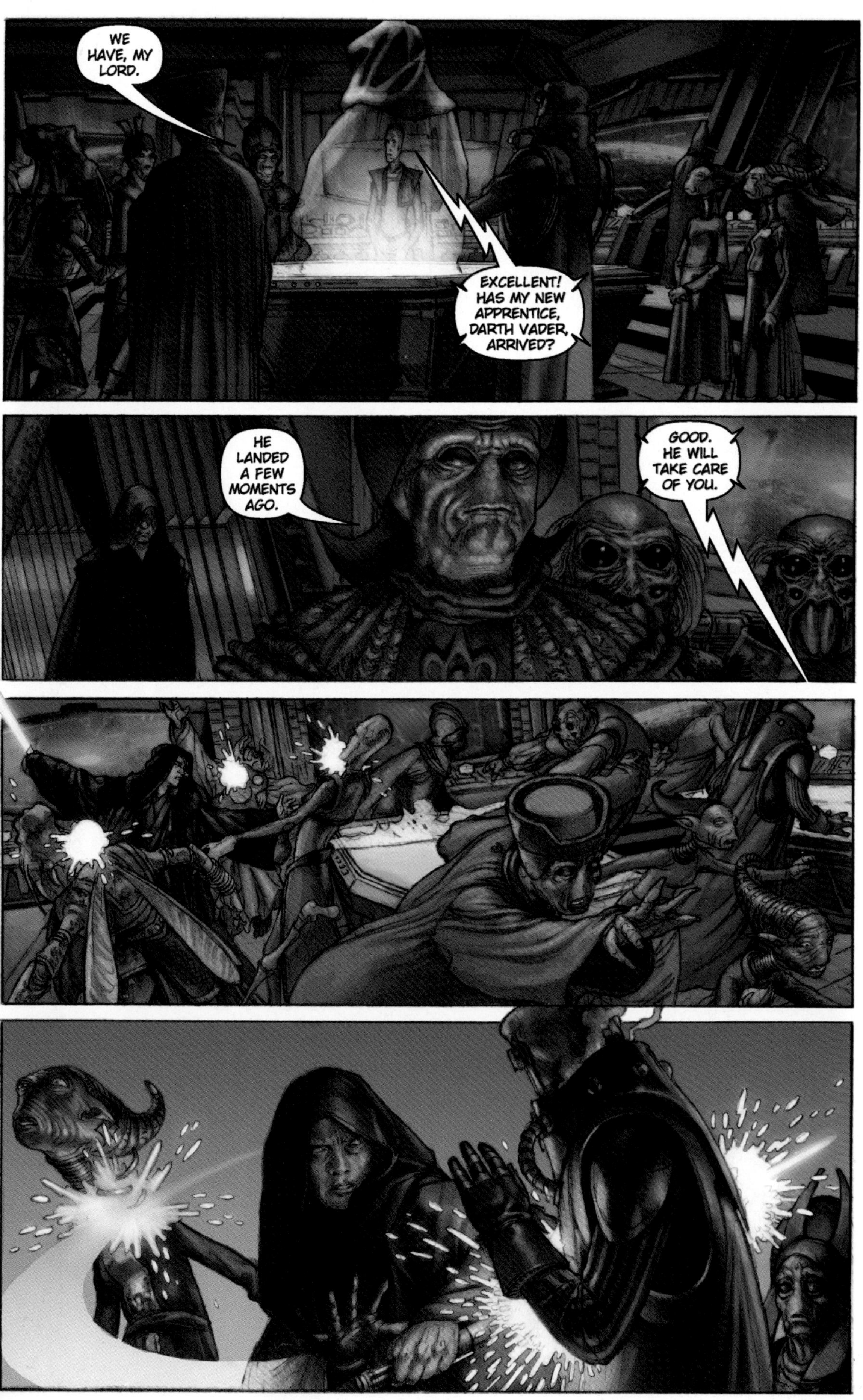
WE HAVE, MY LORD.
EXCELLENT! HAS MY NEW APPRENTICE, DARTH VADER, ARRIVED?
HE LANDED A FEW MOMENTS AGO.
GOOD. HE WILL TAKE CARE OF YOU.

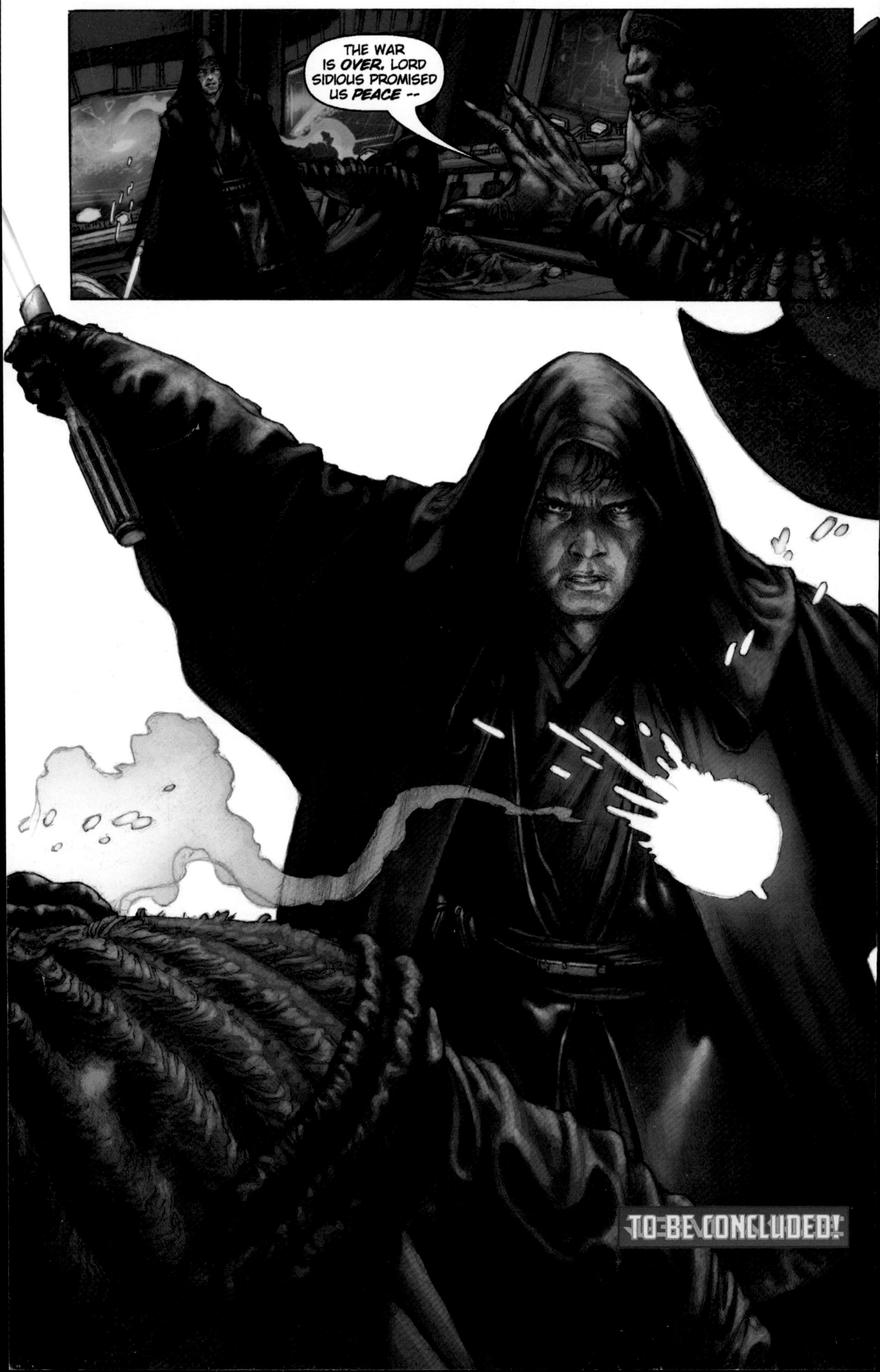
THE WAR IS OVER. LORD SIDIOUS PROMISED US PEACE --
TO BE CONCLUDED!